GOODNIGHT MOON

by Margaret Wise Brown
Pictures by Clement Hurd

TWO HOOTS

In the great green room
There was a telephone
And a red balloon
And a picture of—

The cow jumping over the moon

And there were three little bears sitting on chairs

And two little kittens
And a pair of mittens

And a little toyhouse
And a young mouse

And a comb and a brush and a bowl full of mush

And a quiet old lady who was whispering "hush"

Goodnight room

Goodnight moon

Goodnight cow jumping over the moon

Goodnight light
And the red balloon

Goodnight bears
Goodnight chairs

Goodnight kittens

And goodnight mittens

Goodnight clocks
And goodnight socks

Goodnight little house

And goodnight mouse

Goodnight comb
And goodnight brush

Goodnight nobody

Goodnight mush

And goodnight to the old lady
whispering "hush"

Goodnight stars

Goodnight air

Goodnight noises everywhere

Top tips for helping to get your child to sleep

by HANNAH LOVE, Sleep Consultant

Parents often see getting their child to sleep as a daunting problem to tackle. When parents contact me I reassure them that all children have the ability to sleep well – the most important thing is for the parent to stay relaxed, consistent and confident.

With that in mind and remembering that all children are different, here are my top tips for sleep:

- **Avoid short naps leading up to sleep time.** Even a "power nap" for a couple of moments could prevent your child from falling back to sleep for several hours!

- **"Sleep triggers" are key.** A good bedtime routine could include lullabies or white noise, a soft toy and a comforting book like *Goodnight Moon*.

- **Be realistic and have manageable goals.** If your baby is feeding to sleep don't expect you will move them instantly to falling asleep unaided. Choose a more gradual change and once your child is drifting off without feeding, you can look at ways of moving forward.

- **Bedtime should be a soothing time for everyone.** Children are amazing at picking up on your body language and tone of voice, so try to breathe deeply and talk softly – show that you're calm and they will find it much easier to unwind.

- **Reading should be the last thing you do before sleep.** It is best for the child to be fully ready for bed, with teeth brushed, before snuggling down with *Goodnight Moon* to get them fully settled.

- **Always prepare older babies and toddlers for change.** If you are embarking on any "sleep training" then explain the change you are going to make first – use role play or pictures to make it easy to understand.

- **Books can be one of the best aids to a relaxing bedtime.** Using the same book can be a good idea as children love repetition. The words should indicate that it is sleep time – this will help your child anticipate sleep approaching, which makes it seem less daunting.

Hannah Love (DipHE, DipION) is a sleep consultant, nanny, nutritional therapist, paediatric nurse and mother of three with over 20 years' experience of helping babies and children to fall asleep through her Yummy Baby Group.